A Rainbow of Friends

**Written and illustrated by
P.K. Hallinan**

*For my rainbow of friends—
the children of this earth.*

Ideals Children's Books • Nashville, Tennessee

This edition produced for School Book Fairs.

Copyright © 1994 by P.K. Hallinan

Published by Ideals Children's Books
An imprint of Hambleton-Hill Publishing, Inc.
Nashville, Tennessee 37218

Printed and bound in the U.S.A.

Hallinan, P.K.
    A rainbow of friends / written and illustrated by P.K. Hallinan.
      p.   cm.
    Summary: A story in verse about how all friends are special and valuable
regardless of differences or difficulties.
    ISBN 0-8249-8657-1 (lib.) —ISBN 0-8249-8653-9 (pbk.)
    [1. Friendship—Fiction. 2. Multiculturalism—Fiction. 3. Stories in rhyme.]
I. Title.
    PZ8.3.H15Ra1 1994
    [E]—dc20
                                                  93-39257
                                                  CIP
                                                  AC

A rainbow of friends
is the vision we see
when we think about peace
and world harmony.

Some friends are funny.

Some friends are stars.

Some friends wear clothing
that's different from ours.

But all friends are special
and add in some way
to the richness of life—
how we think, what we say.

A rainbow of friends
is a dream we can share
where everyone's treated
with kindness and care.

A friend may be challenged in movement or speech.

A friend may be distant
or difficult to reach.

Still, each friend is given
a share of our hearts,
so no one feels different,
unloved, or apart.

A rainbow of friends
is a chance for us all
to help one another
when we stumble or fall.

We all have our interests.

We all have our views.

We all have our strengths
and our weaknesses too.

And though we may wander
a bit wide or far,
our friends still accept us
the way that we are.

A rainbow of friends
is a bonding together
that eases our journey
through all kinds of weather.

If we work hand in hand,
all jobs can be done.

Our goals can be reached
with the greatest success
by trusting that others
are doing their best.

So reach out with love
to the people you meet,
and offer a smile
to all those you greet.

on a rainbow of friends.